Where's the Gold.

'AAARRK!
Where's the gold?
I'm so c-c-c-c-c-c-c-cold,'
screeched the green parrot.

**Where's the Gold? Can you help three
brave pirates and their noisy parrot find it?**

For Deborah Brush

PUFFIN BOOKS

Published by the Penguin Group
Penguin Group (Australia)
250 Camberwell Road
Camberwell, Victoria 3124, Australia
(a division of Pearson Australia Group Pty Ltd)
Penguin Group (USA) Inc.
375 Hudson Street, New York, New York 10014, USA
Penguin Group (Canada)
90 Eglinton Avenue East, Suite 700,
Toronto ON M4P 2Y3, Canada
(a division of Pearson Penguin Canada Inc.)
Penguin Books Ltd
80 Strand, London WC2R 0RL, England
Penguin Ireland
25 St Stephen's Green, Dublin 2, Ireland
(a division of Penguin Books Ltd)
Penguin Books India Pvt Ltd
11, Community Centre, Panchsheel Park, New Delhi-110 017, India
Penguin Group (NZ)
67 Apollo Drive, Rosedale, North Shore 0632, New Zealand
(a division of Pearson New Zealand Ltd)
Penguin Books (South Africa) (Pty) Ltd
24 Sturdee Avenue, Rosebank, Johannesburg 2196, South Africa

Penguin Books Ltd, Registered Offices: 80 Strand, London WC2R 0RL, England

First published by Penguin Group (Australia), 2005
This paperback edition published by Penguin Group (Australia), 2010

10 9 8 7 6 5 4

Text and illustrations copyright © Pamela Allen, 2005

The moral right of the author and illustrator has been asserted.

Design by Deborah Brash © Penguin Group (Australia)
Typeset in 22pt Garth Graphic by Deborah Brash
Colour reproduction by Splitting Image, Clayton, Victoria
Printed in China by Everbest Printing Co Ltd

National Library of Australia
Cataloguing-in-Publication data:

Allen, Pamela.
Where's the gold?

ISBN 978 0 14 350147 3

1. Treasure-trove – Juvenile fiction. I. Title.

A823.3

puffin.com.au

Where's the Gold?

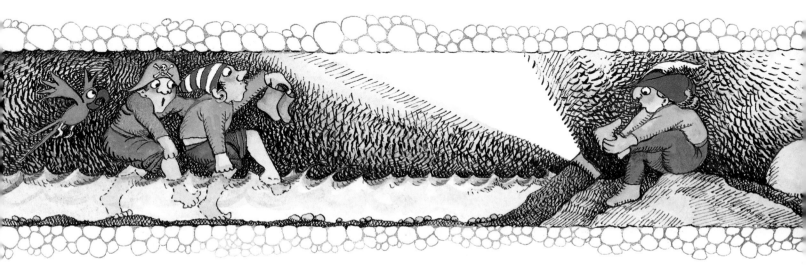

Pamela Allen

PUFFIN BOOKS

Happiness is not getting what you want,

But wanting what you have got.

Here are three pirates brave and bold,
Jeremy, Bellamy and Ted.

They rowed ashore to look for gold.
Jeremy, Bellamy and Ted.

Can you tell them where to look?

'AAARRK!'
screeched the green parrot.

They beached the boat to look around.
Jeremy, Bellamy and Ted.

They climbed a hill
and there they found
a big deep hole in the ground.

'It's dark,' said Jeremy.
'And damp,' murmured Bellamy.
'It's dark. It's damp. And it's *dirty*,' said Ted.

'AAARRK!'
screeched the green parrot.

Then one by one,
through the hole
and down the rope,
dangling dangerously
they dropped.

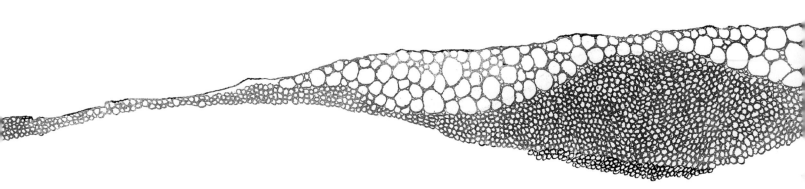

Through the hole
down the rope
and along the tunnel,
cold and cramped they crept.

'AAARRK!
I'm so c-c-c-c-c-c-cold,'
screeched the green parrot.

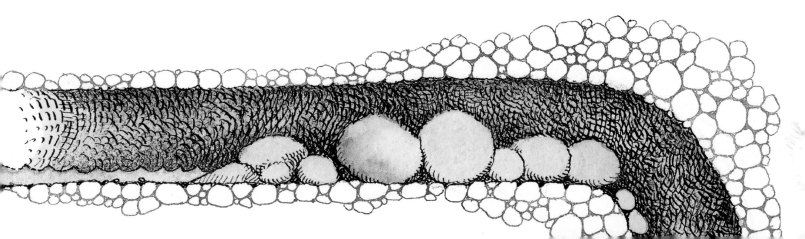

Through the hole
down the rope
along the tunnel
and into the water,
shloshing and shivering they stepped.

'AAARRK!
I'm so c-c-c-c-c-c-cold.
Where's the gold?'
screeched the green parrot.

Through the hole
down the rope
along the tunnel
into the water
and over the boulders,
clawing and clutching
they clambered.

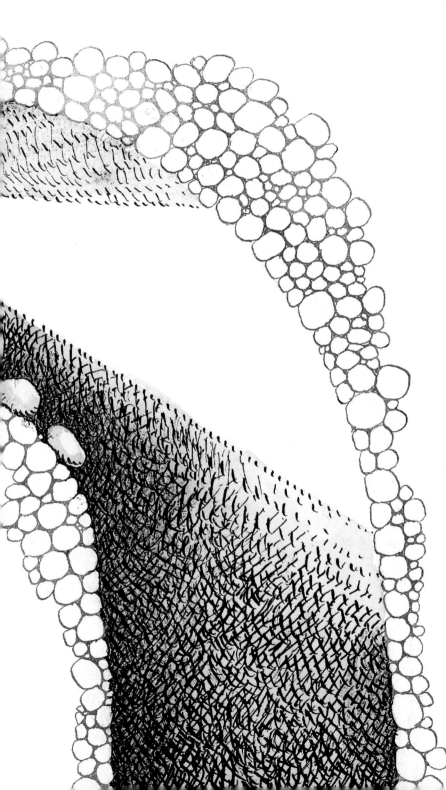

'AAARRK!
Where's the gold?'
screeched the
green parrot.

Through the hole
down the rope
along the tunnel
into the water
over the boulders
and around the corner,
carefully and quietly
they crept.

Suddenly . . .
they all were stopped.
Up ahead the way was blocked.
'Shhhhh!' whispered Jeremy.
'Listen . . .
There's something there.'

'Oooh!' whimpered Ted.
'I don't feel well,
I don't feel well.'

'AAARRK!
I'm so c-c-c-c-c-c-cold.
Where's the gold?'
screeched the green parrot.

'Shhhhh!' hissed Jeremy.
'I think it's sleeping.'
 Cautiously, they kept on creeping.

'What can you see?'
 whispered Bellamy.

Jeremy shivered.
'It's something scary.
 It's big and black and very hairy.'

'AAARRK!
I will fight! I can b-b-b-b-b-b-b-bite!'
screeched the green parrot.

'Shhhhhhhhh!
Listen!'

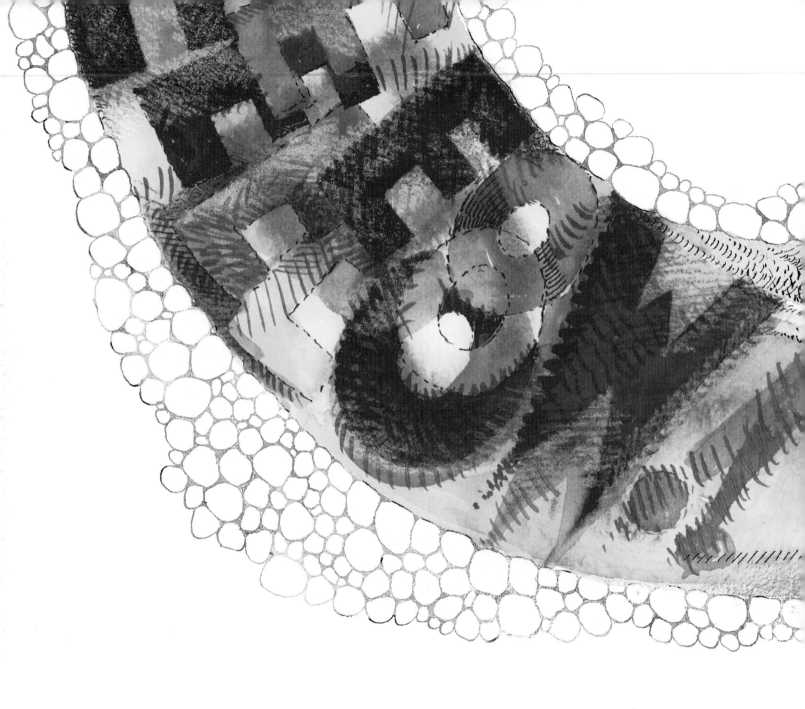

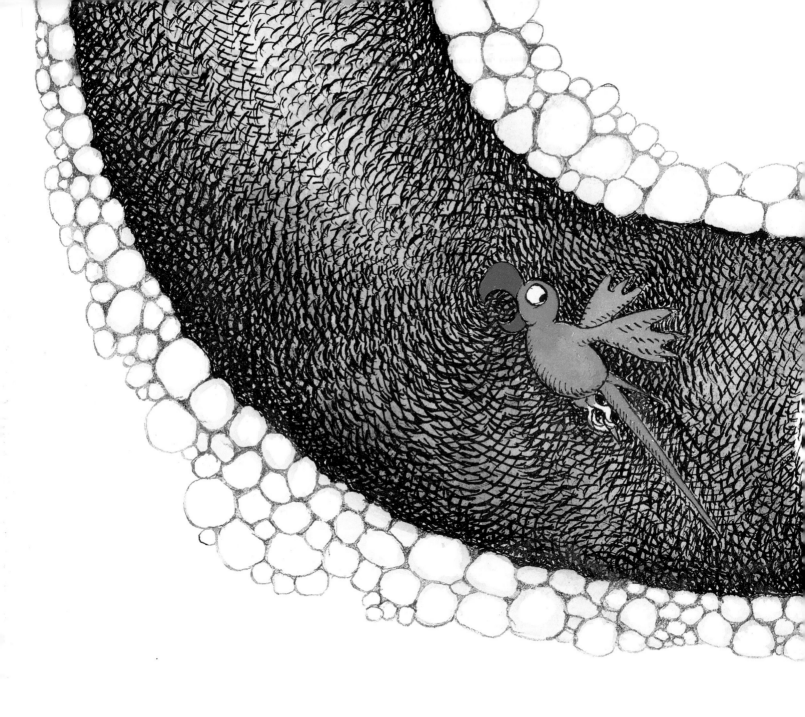

Back they ran
as fast as they could
around the corner,

around the corner
and over the boulders,

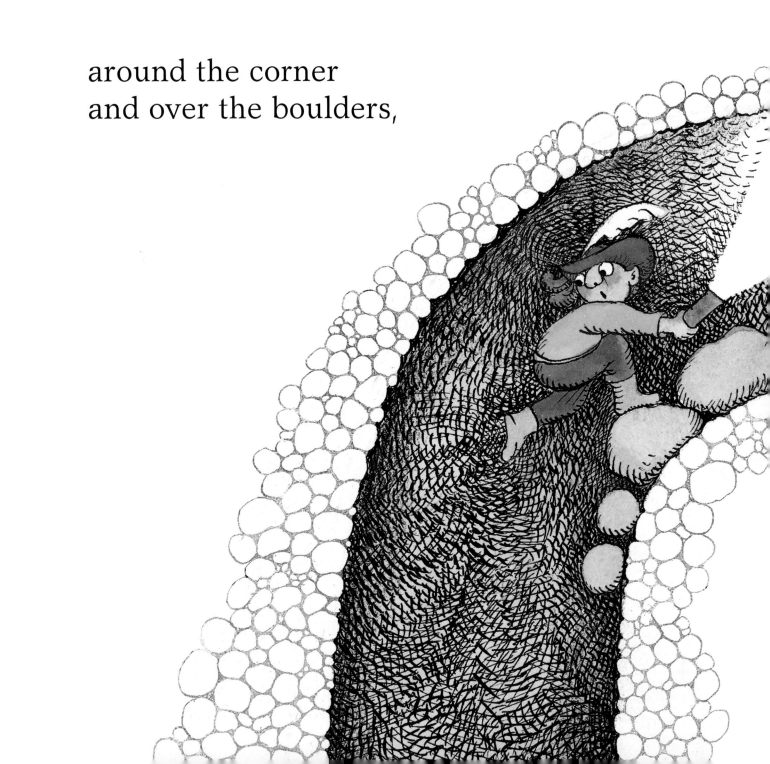

over the boulders
and into the water,

out of the water
and along the tunnel,

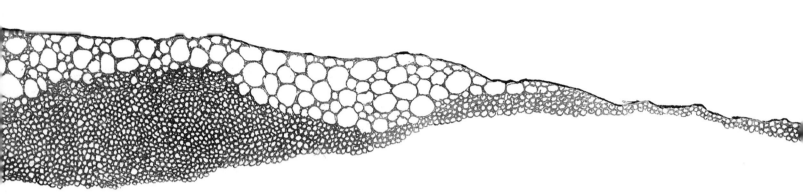

along the tunnel
and up the rope,

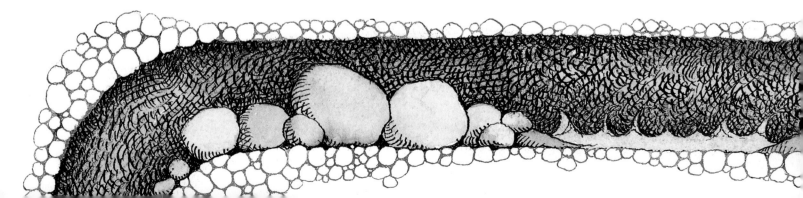

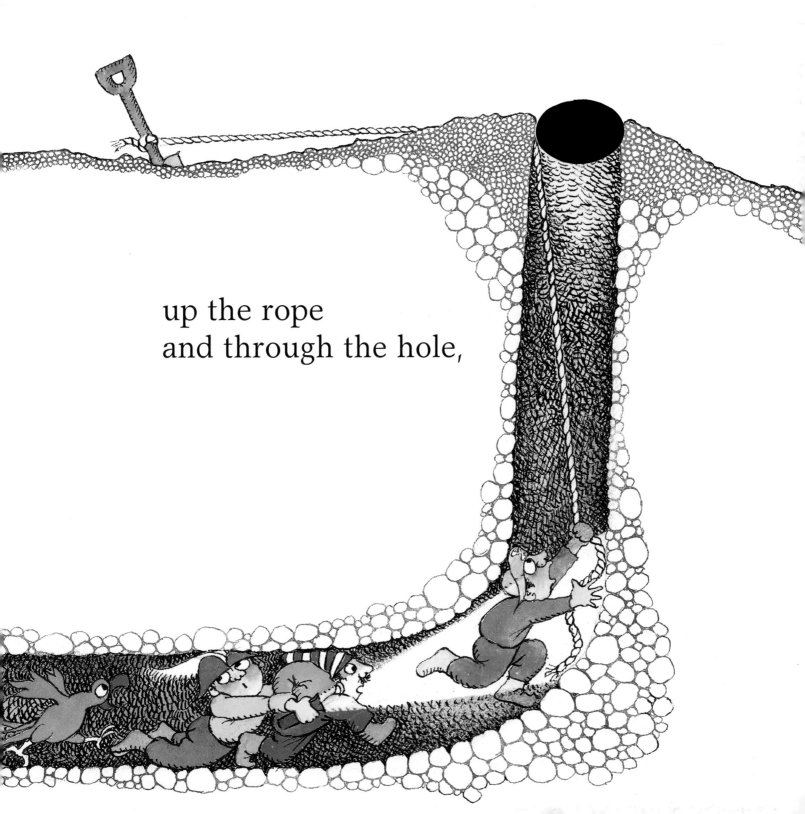

up the rope
and through the hole,

through the hole
and down the hill,

down the hill
and into the boat,

ran Jeremy, Bellamy and Ted.

'AAARRK!
The gold! The gold!
Here's the gold!'
screeched the green parrot.

Here's the gold!